Dream On, Daisy!

Jenny Oldfield

Illustrated by
Lauren Child

Hodder
Children's
Books

a division of Hodder Headline Limited

For Scott and Luke

First published in Great Britain in 2001
by Hodder Children's Books

10 9 8 7 6 5 4 3

A Catalogue record for this book is available from
the British Library

ISBN 0 340 85078 7

Printed and bound in Great Britain
by Bookmarque Ltd, Croydon, Surrey

The paper and board used in this paperback by Hodder Children's
Books are natural recyclable products made from wood grown in
sustainable forests. The manufacturing processes conform to the
environmental regulations of the country of origin.

Hodder Children's Books
a division of Hodder Headline Ltd
338 Euston Road
London NW1 3BH

Contents

Leave it out, Lennox!

One

'Jimmy, don't forget your jacket! Maya, stop dithering! Nathan, comb your hair before we leave!' Miss Ambler fired off last-minute orders. She was leading the school trip to Wakeley Abbey. Do-this, do-that, and don't-you-dare-step-out-of-line!

Daisy Morelli glared out of the classroom window. *Scabby old Wakeley Abbey with Miss Boring-Snoring! Huh!* Other kids went to safari parks where lions roared. *Rrrraaaaagghhh!* Or they rode the speeding, swooping, soaring Spacebuster at Waterland.

Neeeeyaah-sploosh! Wet and gasping, white and weak-kneed. *That* was what Daisy called a good day out.

But no. Their class was stuck with the scabby abbey. A pile of old stones by a river. Sheep munching the grass in the graveyard. Ambler wittering on about King Henry the Eighth.

'Can you sneak your footie on to the coach?' Daisy whispered to her best friend, Jimmy Black. Then at least they'd be able to kick a ball around during lunch.

Jimmy nodded and winked. He tapped his bulging rucksack. Skinny, football-mad Jimmy had already thought of that.

'Daisy, stop whispering!' Miss Ambler barked. 'And Leonie, lead the way!'

Single file down the corridor, left-right, left-right. Turn left past the hall, quick march. Straight out of the main exit. Silence! Thirty kids headed out into the bright sunshine of a June morning.

'Jimmy, I thought I told you to bring your

jacket in case it rains,' the teacher nattered, spying him in his blue-and-white Steelers kit. Luckily, she didn't notice the round bulge in his bag.

'Miss, I left it at home,' he told her shyly. Ambler tutted and let him off. 'Daisy, didn't I tell you to comb your hair?' she said crossly, spying her least favourite pupil's wild black mane further back in the line.

'No, Miss, that was Nathan!'

Nathan Moss, with his messy birds' nest hair, his taped glasses, freckles and mega-brain.

Nathan gave her a sharp kick from behind.

'Ouch!' Daisy cried.

'Daisy, do be quiet!' Ambler sighed wearily before she strode off to the front of the crocodile. 'Quick march across the playground!' she told her class. 'The bus should be waiting at the gate. Now children, remember – best behaviour from each and every one, including Daisy Morelli. The good name of Woodbridge Junior is at stake!'

Hitch number one, no bus at the gate.

'Well, this *is* Friday the thirteenth,' Leonie Flowers pointed out. 'Who in their right mind would arrange a school trip for Friday the thirteenth?'

A wild-eyed Miss Ambler dashed back across the playground to the secretary's office to make a phone call.

'Don't worry, the bus will get here soon,' Winona Jones chipped in with her smug smile.

'Oh, yeah, Winona! Like, you know everything!' Daisy scoffed.

Winona tossed her shiny golden curls. 'As a matter of fact, Daisy Morelli, my mum is on that bus helping the driver to find the school. She offered to help out for the day. And she knows these streets, so there!'

Daisy frowned and groaned. Mizz Smarmy-Smarty Pants. Win-oh-na was nine going on fifty. And her mother was worse.

'Come on, Jim, get out your football while we're waiting,' Leonie suggested.

Jimmy grinned. He unzipped his bag, grabbed the ball and passed it neatly to Leonie. She dribbled it between the netball post and the stone wall, then tapped it towards Daisy.

'Oh, and Morelli's half asleep out there on the left wing!' Jimmy cried in a breathless TV commentator's voice. 'The Steelers' latest international signing from Rome looks slow off the mark. I wonder, will Steelers' manager, Kevin Crowe, already be regretting the multi-million pound deal?'

Morelli heard the crowd boo. The noise rose from the terraces like the cry of a sick cow. Her first game for her high-flying new club, first touch of the ball, and already the home fans had turned against her. It didn't matter to them that she was homesick for Roma, for her poppa's pizzas and her momma's pasta. All they were interested in was her scoring goals.

So she put on a burst of speed, tackled

Flowers and took the ball back. Now she had it out on the left wing and was dribbling smoothly past the defence towards the goalmouth.

'Morelli, Morelli!' the crowd began to chant, slowly at first, then faster.

Past two defenders, with the goal in sight. Only the keeper stood between the new signing and glory. Morelli narrowed her eyes and aimed. Bam! The ball exploded from the tip of her right foot into the back of the net.

'Yeeeeeaaah!' the crowd yelled and screamed. They hugged and threw their hats in the air.

Morelli punched a victory salute, turned and trotted downfield...

... Straight into Miss Ambler! 'Daisy, what on earth are you doing now?' the exasperated teacher cried. She'd returned from her phone call with the news that the bus was on its way. And she'd found Daisy prancing like a maniac in the middle of the playground.

Daisy snuck a look at Jimmy and Leonie. They stood with their backs to the wall, smiling innocently. There was no ball in sight. 'Erm, I was just practisin', Miss!' she stuttered.

'Practising *what*, may I ask?' Ambler quizzed.

'Erm, line dancing, Miss!' Daisy flushed bright red.

'Ah, yes, line dancing. Funny, I never had you down as a dancer, Daisy. Still, the world is full of surprises. Very nice, dear.' Luckily, the scatty teacher's attention was drawn towards the arrival of a white coach and she dashed off.

'Line dancing!' Jimmy giggled.

Daisy glared back. 'A fat lot of help you were!'

He held up the ball from behind his back. 'I've still got this, haven't I?'

But not for long. With a snarl and a snap of teeth, Fat Lennox snatched Jimmy's precious footie. The dog had appeared from nowhere, his stocky white body hurtling through the air. He sank his fangs into the plastic ball.

Hisssss!

Jimmy, Leonie and Daisy stared in horror.

Sssss! Flat as a pancake. Gurgling and choking, Lennox dropped the useless object to the ground and trampled on it. *Huff-huff-huff,* he coughed.

'Oh, great!' Leonie stood with her hands on her hips. 'Trust Fat Lennox!'

Fat Lennox belonged to the school caretaker, Bernie King. The white bulldog slavered and waddled and had evil little red-rimmed eyes.

'Look what he did to my footie!' Jimmy wailed.

Miss Ambler was by now counting everyone on to the coach. She yelled for the stragglers still in the playground to hurry up.

'*Now* what do we do during our lunchbreak?' Leonie demanded in disgust.

Daisy's mind was working fast. OK, so soccer was out. But it might be fun... it would mean smuggling him on to the bus in secret, of course... no one else must know... not that he was the friendliest animal in the world either... exactly the opposite, in fact... but still, he *was* better than nothing...

'Why don't we take Lennox with us?' she suggested. 'Let's not tell Ambler, or Bernie, or anybody. We can just stow him away in the boot!'

Two

'You grab Miss Ambler's attention,' Daisy told Leonie. 'Jimmy and me will smuggle Lennox on board!'

'What if he won't come with us?' Jimmy asked nervously.

He, Leonie and Daisy were the only ones left in the playground, not counting Bernie King's fat dog. They could hear the teacher counting heads on the bus – 'Twenty-one, twenty-two, twenty-three...'

Daisy's eyes sparkled. 'He will!' she promised, taking a chocolate bar out of her pocket. Lennox's own eyes lit up and his jaw went slack. 'Nice choccy!' Daisy tempted him towards the gate.

'What if Miss Ambler sees us?' Jimmy stammered.

'She won't!' Daisy trusted Leonie to play her part. She might look like butter wouldn't melt, with her halo of dark hair and her shiny white smile, but when a situation called for sneaky tactics, Leonie was first choice.

'Give me ten seconds,' Ambler's golden girl muttered, nipping out through the gate.

'C'mon, Lennox, let's move it!' Daisy hissed.The dog drooled as she waved the chocolate in his face.

'Now, has everyone handed over their lunches so that they can be safely stowed in the luggage hold?' the teacher was asking in her high-pitched voice.

'Yes, Miss!' came the chorus.

'Leonie, what is it?' Daisy and Jimmy overheard Ambler ask. 'You're pointing to something under my seat, but I can't hear a word you say.'

'Please, Miss, my pocket money just rolled under there,' Leonie whimpered. 'It's stuck!'

'Here, let me help,' Miss Ambler offered.

'She fell for it!' Jimmy squeaked.

' 'Course she did,' Daisy laughed, turning back to the dog. 'C'mon, Lennox. Nice Lennie – doggy-choccy!'

Backing out through the gate, with Jimmy shooing the pooch from behind, Daisy snuck out on to the pavement. *Plod-plod* – the bulldog padded after her. 'Lovely, gooey choccy!' Daisy felt the bar melt in the heat of the sun. 'Yum-yum!'

Slobbering and slavering, stumbling on his short legs, Lennox followed her alongside the bus.

'Jimmy, get on the coach this minute!' a different voice called. He jumped, then stood to attention. When Winona's mum gave an order, you obeyed.

Daisy's friend had been spotted, but not Daisy. 'Gotta go!' Jimmy hissed, leaving her to cope with Lennox alone. She already had the dog half-in, half-out of the big, dark space where passengers' luggage was kept. Today though, only one corner was full, stacked with colourful lunch boxes and small rucksacks. There was plenty of room for a stowaway dog.

'In here, Lennie!' Daisy whispered. She clambered into the hold and dangled the chocolate in front of him.

Whumph! Lennox reached up, opened his jaws and closed them on empty air. Daisy had snatched her hand away just in time.

'C'mon!' she urged, dangling again.

Urrrumph! Slowly, wheezily, Fat Lennox climbed in after her.

'Good boy!' she sighed, edging around until she was nearest the exit. She swung the chocolate to and fro between her fingers, like a hypnotist putting her victim into a deep sleep. 'You stay here with the nice choccy. I'm going to get out and slam this door down tight shut. Like so!'

Wiping her messy fingers on her clean white T-shirt, Daisy turned and came face to face with Winona.

'What are you up to?' Winona asked, her eyes narrowed, her nose twitching like a curious pointy-faced shrew. *Upon my whiskers, I'm sure something strange is going on!*

'Nothing. I'm closing the door to save the driver a job, that's all!' Daisy defended herself. *Keep quiet, Lennox!* she prayed. If Winona found out that the dog was a stowaway, she would be bound to give the game away.

Winona's blue eyes bored straight through her.

Wrrrrruffff!

'What was that?' Winona heard the muffled sound and reached out for the handle to the luggage hold.

'Nothing! It was the engine. I think the driver's ready to leave!' Daisy said desperately.

Wrrruuuuggggh!

Winona tutted. 'No way was that the

engine!' She began to turn the handle.

'Winona, Daisy, come here at once!' Mrs Jones leaned out of the door and screeched her order. A wind came along and whipped up her carefully gelled, pale blonde hair. Her head looked like a gone-wrong meringue.

The girls dropped everything and ran for the steps. Once inside, the driver swished the doors closed behind them.

'Sit down next to Jimmy!' Mrs Jones glared at Daisy. Then, 'Winona, dear, you come and sit at the front with me,' she cooed at her own darling child.

Winona's pointy-shrew face glared at Daisy behind her mum's back. 'Just you wait till we get to the abbey,' she hissed. 'I'll soon find out what you were up to, Daisy Morelli!'

'Here it is, Miss!' Leonie broke in, scrabbling out from under a seat and holding up a pound coin. 'It rolled halfway down the coach!'

Miss Ambler emerged from underneath the seat in front, her long, wispy hair straggled over her red cheeks. 'See, I knew there was no need to worry!' she blinked through her steamed-up glasses. 'Things always turn up if you look hard enough.'

'Ready?' the driver grunted, waiting for everyone to settle in their seats.

'Drive on!' Mrs Jones said with a sweep of her hand. 'Next stop, Wakeley Abbey, if you please!'

'The Abbey was built in the thirteenth century by the monks of the Cistercian order...' Mrs Jones's voice droned on throughout the long journey. It turned out she was even more of an expert on abbeys than Rambler-Ambler.

'The Sister-what?' Daisy mumbled.

'The Sister Shuns,' Jimmy answered. 'Maybe they were a type of nun or something.'

From the seats behind, Leonie giggled and Nathan scoffed. 'The Cistercians,' he told them. 'They were monks, as in *men*, not women.'

'Yeah, but they wore long dresses,' Leonie added. 'So it's an easy mistake to make!'

Soon the back row of the bus started to sing to try and drown out Mrs Jones. The latest boy band single took over from monks and cloisters. Then someone halfway down the bus said they felt sick. Miss Ambler made a sick-bag out of the plastic wallet containing the list of pupils on the outing.

'Just another wonderful school trip!' Daisy sighed.

'Friday the thirteenth!' Leonie reminded them darkly. 'Expect the worst!'

Suddenly, from the front of the bus, a mobile phone chirruped. The whole class stopped singing and being sick in order to listen in on Miss Ambler's call.

'Oh, hello, Mr King... yes, we're out for the day on a trip to Wakeley Abbey... why, what's wrong?'

Jimmy shot Daisy a worried look. She stared straight ahead at the sign welcoming them to the ancient abbey.

'No, I'm afraid I haven't seen Lennox, Mr King... I'm sorry that you've lost him, but I'm sure he'll soon turn up... Yes, I'm absolutely certain that your dog is not aboard this bus. Goodbye!'

Phew! Daisy breathed again. Anyway, it was too late to turn back now. Even when Ambler did discover Lennox in the luggage hold, they would have to keep him with them for the day. She looked forward to the chubby dog getting up to all sorts of mischief.

At last the driver pulled up in the car park and opened the doors to let the kids tumble out.

'Best behaviour!' Rambler-Ambler reminded them. But her voice was lost in the whoops and cries.

Then dainty Mrs Jones descended. She minced on her high heels to get the pupils' lunches from the hold.

Wrrruuufff! The bulldog greeted her with a pleased bark and a schlep and schlop of his slobbery jaws.

'What... is... *that*?' prim Mrs Jones cried in disgust.

Miss Ambler ran to see the trampled, torn, squished packed lunches inside the hold. Even from a safe distance, Daisy could see that the dog had eaten everything he could sink his teeth into. His cheeks bulged and his stomach had blown up like a balloon.

'Oh my, that's Lennox!' the teacher wailed.

Fat Lennox. *Very* Fat Lennox! Sitting there, full of stolen sandwiches. And boy, did he look glad the bus had arrived!

Three

For a moment, Daisy thought Lennox was about to do the sick trick. The bloated dog blinked in the light and made a suspicious choking sound.

'Whoah, stand well back,' the driver advised. 'Give the stowaway breathing space!'

Groggy from the long sea voyage, the convict peered from the dark hold. His eyes were red, his legs weak and trembling.

'Avast, me hearties!' the pirate captain

cried. 'What have we here?'

Midshipman Daisy drew her curved cutlass and glared at the stowaway with her one good eye. 'Shall I slit 'is throat, cap'n?' she growled.

Fat Lennox went down on his knees. 'Spare me!' he croaked. 'I have a thousand gold coins in my pockets. You can have five hundred if you spare my life!'

Daisy pointed the tip of her sword at the fat man's chest. 'If we kill you and toss you overboard, we keep the whole thousand!' she sneered nastily, adjusting the black patch over her bad eye.

The convict's teeth chattered. 'N-no, p-please!'

'Only kidding!' Midshipman Daisy lowered her sword. 'Why not join our pirate gang instead? Sail the waves, help us plunder and swashbuckle and tear the livers out of all the lousy landlubbers we can find!'

All of a sudden, Lennox jumped out of the luggage hold. He landed heavily at Miss Ambler's feet. 'Oh my!' she gasped.

The dog shook his head and made his floppy cheeks wobble.

Winona skipped out of the way of the spray from Lennox's mouth.

'We must call Mr King!' Mrs Jones made a snap decision, delving into her bag for her phone and punching in the school number.

'Miss, he ate my sandwiches! Miss, the dog stole my lunch!' the kids wailed.

'Quiet!' Mrs Jones snapped.

'However did he get in there in the first place?' poor, shell-shocked Miss Ambler cried. She looked from Jimmy to Leonie to Nathan.

'I haven't got a clue,' Nathan said with a shrug.

'Daisy?' The teacher's eye fixed on the trouble magnet.

Daisy stared back, wide-eyed.

'Yeah, Daisy!' Winona muttered under her

breath. So this was what all that strange stuff with the luggage hold had been about!

But before Winona could go on, Leonie stepped smartly on her shiny black shoe. 'Don't say a word!' she warned, without moving her lips.

Winona gritted her teeth. 'Ouch! – OK, I promise.' Pulling her foot free, she hopped away.

By this time, Winona's mum had got through to Bernie King. 'Mr King, we can put your mind at rest. Lennox is with us after all. He stowed away in the boot, and he's here at Wakeley Abbey... No, we don't know exactly how it happened. But don't worry, we'll take very good care of him.'

Daisy grinned at Jimmy and Leonie.

'Miss Ambler, may I look after Lennox for the day?' Leonie asked sweetly. 'I'll make sure he doesn't get into trouble.'

With a sigh, Miss Ambler agreed. 'Very well, Leonie dear. Where's my list? Whose camera is this? Kyle, blow your nose, Jade, look where you're going, Maya, don't lag behind!'

'Cool!' Daisy beamed at Leonie then attacked Jimmy's rucksack. 'Lend me this strap,' she insisted. 'Look, the sign over there says you have to keep dogs on a lead!'

'Don't rip it!' he told her.

Too late. With a quick yank, Daisy tore the strap clean off. Then she slotted it through Lennox's studded collar.

Hrrrufff! he snarled.

'Be a good doggie!' Daisy cooed.

Hrrrruuuufff!

'Oh, leave it out, Lennox!' Leonie warned, grabbing the strap from Daisy and walking the dog down the narrow footpath towards the abbey. 'That growly stuff doesn't impress us. We all know you're a slobbery old softie at heart!'

Plod-plod-plod. Lennox made his lazy way down the sandy footpath. His little eyes blinked and took in the sheep grazing by the river. White woolly things with thin legs and long, dangling tails. Some sturdy lambs skipping through the buttercups. Lennox acted puzzled.

'C'mon, Lennox!' Leonie tugged at the lead. 'They're only sheep.'

'Maybe he never saw one before,' Jimmy suggested. 'He's a city dog, remember.'

Daisy gazed down at the river and up at the blue sky. Tufts of white cloud drifted by. Below them, the ruined abbey looked grey and big-time boring. A couple of arches, a few crumbling walls, a roof. *Yawn-yawn.*

Meanwhile, a steady stream of kids walked two by two, led by Mrs Jones and Miss Ambler.

'Hey, Lennox, I said c'mon!' Leonie insisted with a frown.

The caretaker's bulldog had sat down and refused to budge. One wicked little eye was still fixed on the distant sheep.

'C'mon, you big lummox!' Leonie cried.

'What's a lumm...?' Jimmy hadn't got the word out before Fat Lennox gave a giant leap.

He tugged the strap clean out of Leonie's hand and made a bee-line for the sheep.

Wrrruuffff! Jaws snapping, little legs trundling, he barrelled down the hill.

'Come back!' Leonie called.

'Uh-oh!' Jimmy panicked.

Daisy set off after the runaway dog. She saw big brown birds rise from the long

grass and flap noisily away. She heard Miss Ambler's voice shouting at her, almost drowned out by the roar of water over rocks in the river bed.

Squelch! Lennox raced through a patch of marshy ground and Daisy followed. *Gloop-gloop!* She trod through the mud.

Wrrraaagh! Lennox roared. The lambs leaped straight up in the air, the mother sheep baaed and scattered dizzily. The dog zigzagged between the fleeing sheep, snarling and barking. He trailed his lead in small circles, snapping his teeth and missing his tottering prey.

'Come here!' Daisy ordered. *Whumph!* She made a dive and missed. Picking herself up from the ground, she tried a second time, then a third. Lennox dodged. He sure was fast for a fat dog.

Baa! Baaaa-baaaa! The sheep gave their flat, silly cry.

Lennox ducked a fourth time and Daisy landed splat in something soft.

By now, Leonie had joined in the chase. 'Come here, Lennox!' she said sternly. The dog stopped in his tracks and looked – well, sheepish. 'It's no good acting like that!' Leonie told him, marching towards him and picking up the lead. 'You're a bad boy, and you know it!'

Hufffff! Lennox's head sagged. He trotted meekly after Leonie, who walked quickly to rejoin the group.

'Well done, Leonie!' Miss Ambler cried. 'If we'd left it to Daisy to catch him, we'd have been here until teatime!'

Huh! Daisy gazed down at her smeared T-shirt. It was covered in green and brown stains. Her mum would kill her when she got home. And yet this was all the thanks she got.

Now it was time for them to go into the abbey, Rambler-Ambler announced, wiping her hands of messy Daisy.

Daisy wiped her own hands on her already dirty top and deliberately lagged behind. *Who wants to know about monks chanting and growing their own vegetables?* she asked herself. Mrs Jones was firing useless facts at the group, pointing to what was left of the walls. *Will they notice if I kind of disappear and do my own thing?* she wondered.

Why not risk it? a little voice inside her head asked.

I'll be in big trouble if I get caught, Daisy told the voice.

So what's new?

Yeah, right! Suddenly Daisy decided to get lost. She dropped out of sight behind a pillar, then waited for Mrs Jones's voice to waft away as she led the group down a central aisle. There was a load of low archways off to the right. The sign above them said *Cloisters*. Daisy didn't know what it meant, but it looked like a good place to hide.

Now! the sneaky voice hissed.

Daisy looked to the right and left, saw no one and darted across an open space into the shadow of the old stone arches.

Four

The cloisters smelled damp and musty. Maybe it was the smell of the old, dead monks, Daisy thought. They were silent and, she had to admit, a teeny bit spooky. *So, I could go and find the others*, she said to herself.

Scaredy-cat! the invisible Daisy hissed.

OK, I'll explore a bit more, then I'll find the rest, she decided.

Daisy stepped nervously through the shady stone arches. It was cold and there were worn steps at the end, leading to a tunnel that was blocked by a rusty iron grille. *Dungeons!*

C'mon, abbeys don't have dungeons! the irritating voice reminded her. *They have things called crypts where they put the dead bodies.*

Daisy shivered.

Huuuaaaggghhh! A ghostly breath filled the air. It came from the dark cave beyond the grille. Daisy's skin prickled all over. She froze.

Huaaaaah!

A ghost! Daisy pictured a monk in a long gown. *Or worse, a walking skeleton! Bare bones grinding as he walked, a yellow skull with deep, dark eye holes...*

Huwuuufff! Fat Lennox's face appeared on the other side of the barrier.

'Boo!' Winona cried, stepping out beside him.

Her heart in her mouth, Daisy stared at the so-called ghosts. 'H-h-how did you get in there?' she whispered.

Winona grinned back. 'Easy. There's another entrance from the east side. Hey, Daisy, what's up? You're white as a sheet!'

'Hah, very funny – not!' Daisy thought she even saw a smirk on the bulldog's fat face. She made up a challenge for sneaky Little Mizz Perfect. 'Listen, I dare you two to squeeze through the gap between these bars!'

'And mess up my best skirt? No way!' Winona refused point blank. 'Anyway, look, Lennox is running away again. Rats! I'm supposed to be taking him back to Miss Ambler.'

'Yeah, well watch this!' Daisy replied, sticking her head through the narrow gap,

then twisting to ease her shoulders through.
She was halfway through when she realised
she was stuck.

'Yeah, well, see ya!' Winona chirped. And
she marched Lennox away down the dark
tunnel.

Daisy's eyes popped. She breathed in
deeply to make her body as skinny as
possible. *Jimmy would have made it, no
problem*, she thought. She pushed and
strained to make it through the tiny gap.

Oooooohhhh! Daisy sucked in her breath
and shoved. Finally she popped out the other
side and collapsed on to the ground. 'Made
it!' she gasped.

Then she was up and trotting after Winona
and Lennox. Or, she thought she was. In fact,
it was too dark to see, and she found that the
tunnel split off in two different directions.
'Which way now?' she said out loud, trying not
to think of spiders and worms – millions of
them creeping and squirming through the
tunnel – moths and bats; earwigs; billions,

trillions of creepy-crawlies...

'Boo!' Winona cried again, popping out from behind a giant stone chest.

'Aaagh!' Daisy's heart hammered against her ribs. 'Leave it out, Winona!' she snapped. Anyway, what are you doing back there? Won't you mess up your nice new skirt?'

'I know, but stupid Lennox decided to crawl under this big grave, and now he won't come out,' Winona grumbled.

'Maybe he's doing his usual trick and digging for bones!' Daisy said darkly. She stared at the stone chest and the faint outline of a long statue lying flat on top.

'Don't just stand there – help!' Winona pleaded.

So Daisy crouched down and tweeted, 'Here, Lennox. C'mon out, there's a good boy!'

Grrrrruuuufff! (Where's the chocolate?)

'C'mon, be good!' Daisy squirmed further behind the ancient tomb.

(Not without the chocolate!) *Rrrruuugh!*

'And here is the tomb of Sir Henry Fah-kwah!' Mrs Jones was announcing as she led the class down into the crypt. 'Fah-kwah, spelt F-A-R-Q-U-H-A-R. Sir Henry had three wives and twelve children, who are all buried in the Fah-kwah tomb right here to your left...'

Lennox shot out from behind the grave like a white cannonball.

'Aaagh! Help! It's a ghost! Miss, I feel sick!' The crypt echoed with the kids' shrieks, cries and groans.

Then Daisy and Winona emerged more slowly. Miss Ambler shone a torch on Daisy's face. 'I might have known!' she sighed. 'Daisy Disaster Morelli strikes again!'

'Jimmy, come away from those stepping-stones! Maya, don't give Lennox any more of your lunch! Nathan, you'll fall from that tree if you're not careful!' Poor Mizz Tizz was a nervous wreck by the time the class reached the riverbank. The plan was to sit on the grass and eat what was left of lunch after Lennox's secret feast.

'Don't worry, Jade dear,' Mrs Jones was still explaining to one of the more nervous pupils. 'There's no such thing as ghosts. That was only Daisy Morelli playing a silly trick on us!'

Daisy ignored them all. She went to join Jimmy by the worn stepping-stones. 'Some school trip this is turning out to be!' she grumbled.

Jimmy balanced on the first stone, judging the distance to the next one in the row. 'What's up? Aren't you having a good time?' he asked, watching the water swirl on either side of the uneven stones.

'Boring old abbey!' Daisy muttered. Her ribs were sore, and she was starving hungry, thanks to Bernie King's dog. 'Whose brilliant idea was it to bring Lennox?' she mumbled, shoving his wet nose away. The pesky dog had recently decided to follow her everywhere.

Grrruuufff! (More choccy, please!)

'Leave it out!' she muttered for the fifteenth time.

'Try this!' Jimmy invited, hopping from the first to the second stone like a little sparrow. 'It's cool!'

So Daisy balanced on the first flat stone. She saw the water rush by, dragging green weeds with it. As Jimmy jumped on to the third stone, she made ready to leap after him.

'Daisy, Jimmy! Come back!' Winona yelled from the shore. 'Didn't you hear Miss Ambler? She said, "Keep off the stepping-stones. They're dangerous!"'

'Avast, me hearties!' Captain Cutlass cried. 'There's treasure on that there island, make no mistake! Gold and silver, diamonds as big as your fist!'

Midshipman Daisy felt the wind in her hair. 'Aye, aye, cap'n!' she yelled as she faced the ocean's mighty swell. She followed Cabin Boy Jim into the eye of the storm.

'Come back, Daisy!' Winona whined. Daisy

was on stone number five. Jimmy was on seven. The current swept by in a rush of bubbles and white foam.

'Oh, no!' From the bank, Winona set up a high wail. 'Now look what you've done!'

Daisy glanced over her shoulder. 'Hold it, Jimmy!' she cried. Turning gingerly on her stone, she saw Fat Lennox launch himself on to the first stone. The dog's short legs only just made it.

'Go back!' Daisy commanded, frantically waving her arms. From the second stone he wagged his stumpy tail and drooled.

Grrrrummph! (Nice choccy! More, more!)

'No, Lennox, please!' Daisy closed her eyes as he prepared to jump again.

The dog leaned back on his haunches, then leaped.

Splash! Right into the river.

'Miss!' Winona screamed wildly. 'Fat Lennox is drowning. Come quick!'

Five

Lennox plunged into the water and vanished. Then his flat head bobbed clear, red eyes streaming, a gurgling sound escaping from his throat.

Daisy and Jimmy froze on their rocks as Winona dashed back to the teacher to deliver the bad news. They watched Lennox paddle his front feet and try to steer for the bank. But the strong current took hold of him and swept him downstream.

For once, Winona wasn't exaggerating, Daisy realised. Fat Lennox was in big trouble.

'Don't panic!' Jimmy cried. Without a thought for his own safety, he jumped from his stone and began to swim to the rescue.

As luck would have it, another current took hold of the boy hero and carried him away from the drowning dog. Daisy watched Jimmy's thin arms doing a frantic crawl through the water, only to be swept in the opposite direction. Within seconds, the current had dumped him on the near bank, and Miss Ambler and Mrs Jones were dragging him on to dry land.

Mrs Jones told everyone to stand back while she gave poor Jim first-aid. 'I may need to give him the kiss of life!' she announced.

At which Jimmy sat bolt upright, spat out some water and said he was fine, thanks.

Back to Lennox, Daisy thought. She saw his white head bobbing across the river towards the far bank and decided against a cold plunge. Better to scoot across the stepping-stones, leap on to dry land and race to cut him off. But she would have to be quick.

So she jumped nimbly from one stone to the next – eleven, twelve, thirteen – right up to twenty-two. *Those monks must have been acrobats*, she thought as, gasping, she reached the far bank. Twice she'd almost overbalanced, and once her foot had slipped right in.

By now, Lennox was fighting to keep his head above water. The current was dragging him under and bobbing him back up again like a cork. He barked feebly for help.

'OK, Len, I'm coming!' Daisy called. She sprinted down the bank, over boulders and across narrow streams. She ducked under low tree branches, climbed a fence and raced on.

'Go, Daisy!' Leonie yelled from the abbey side of the river, as Daisy gradually overtook the struggling dog. 'The current's gonna dump him on that little beach just ahead of you!'

Daisy spotted the beach and put on a last burst of speed. Sure enough, Lennox was being carried straight towards her. He saw her and yelped. His short legs paddled like crazy.

Daisy waded knee-deep into the river. She felt the current pull at her feet and the gravel bed give way. For a second she almost toppled over. And Lennox was being whisked by too fast for her to catch hold. She made a grab, missed and clutched at nothing but water and weeds.

'Oh, no!' came the cry from the class. 'Lennox is gonna die!'

But Leonie saw it differently. 'See the low branch just ahead?' she yelled at Daisy. 'Climb along it and try again!'

Soaked to the skin, Daisy waded downstream while the current swept the dog in small circles just out of her reach. She clambered along the branch, feeling it sway under her weight.

'Go, Daisy!' Jimmy joined in Leonie's chant.

Daisy clung to the branch and leaned down towards the water.

Huuurrr-gulp-gurgle! Lennox gazed up at her, knowing that this was his last chance.

Once more, Daisy made a lunge for his collar. Her fingers slipped under the leather band and she heaved.

Uuugghh, what a weight! It almost pulled her from her perch. Lennox's legs paddled in mid-air as she hauled him out. Then, with one last big effort, Daisy lifted him on to the branch.

'What thanks do I get?' she moaned as she told the story for the tenth time. The day at the abbey was over, Daisy sat in the bus back to school surrounded by curious faces. This time it was Maya and Jared who wanted to hear the details.

'I get Lennox up on to my branch,' she repeated in disgust, 'and what does he do? He slobbers all over me!'

'He was saying thank you,' Maya smiled.

'Rather you than me,' Jared added.

'And look at him now!' Daisy protested, pointing to Fat Lennox, who was snoozing on the front seat next to Mrs Jones. 'That's because she gave him doggy chocs!' she explained. 'I'm the one who saved his life, yet now he acts as if I don't even exist!'

'I wonder what Bernie King will say,' Nathan chipped in from two rows back, reminding everyone that the school gates were in sight.

'This is where we do our vanishing trick,' Daisy muttered to Jimmy and Leonie.

'We hope!' they added.

It was the part Daisy definitely wasn't looking forward to. She spied the caretaker waiting at the gates, arms folded, a scowl on his face. His short hair seemed to bristle as the coach drew up beside him.

Bernie was King of Woodbridge Junior. No door was opened, no chair was moved, without his say-so. And, what's more, he didn't like Daisy Disaster Morelli. She hunched down in her seat as Fat Lennox bounded from the bus.

'How come his collar's wet?' Bernie demanded.

'Ah, well, you see...' Miss Ambler began.

'... *In the river ... Almost drowned!*' the caretaker echoed as the kids filed off the bus. '*Daisy Morelli* ...? I might have guessed!'

A big hand seized her as she stepped into the playground. Ungrateful Lennox smirked up at her. *So much for saving your life!* Daisy scowled back.

'No, you don't understand!' the teacher protested feebly.

'I see it as plain as the nose on my face, Miss Ambler. You only have to mention Daisy's name for me to know that she's the cause of all this trouble!'

Copped. Nicked. Found out! Daisy sagged miserably.

Until Mrs Jones stepped forward with a steely look in her blue eyes. 'Put that child down, Mr King!' she said in ringing tones. 'You should be ashamed of yourself for blaming Daisy!'

Daisy blinked twice. Was she hearing this properly? Was Winona's mum really springing to her defence? Mrs Jones stood inside the playground gate, prim and neat as when they'd started out. Her hair was still whisked into a meringue shape and her lipstick was still pink and glossy.

'This girl saved Lennox's life!' she declared. 'If it wasn't for Daisy Morelli, your dog would have drowned!'

'Yeah!' everyone cried. 'That's true. Daisy's the hero!'

'Lennox smuggled *himself* on to the bus!' the Blonde Bombshell went on. 'What's more, he's been very badly behaved all day long, haven't you, you naughty dog?'

Fat Lennox dropped his head and cowered.

'Look 'ere!' Bernie protested.

'No, *you* look here, Mr King! It simply isn't good enough to go around blaming poor Daisy for Lennox's faults. That dog of yours needs proper training not to eat people's lunches and run away all the time. As a matter of fact, when a dog misbehaves, I always blame the owner – don't you, Miss Ambler?'

Daisy took a deep breath.

All the wind seemed to have gone out of

Bernie's lungs. Like Lennox, he sagged and sulked under Mrs Jones's attack. 'Let's forget it, shall we?' he mumbled, turning on his heel and trudging off with his dog.

'Hmm!' Mrs Jones turned kindly to Daisy. 'Now, you run along home and change into dry clothes, dear. And don't worry, I'll be sure to tell the headteacher how brave you were!'

Daisy's brown eyes sparkled as she thanked Mrs Jones and scooted off with Jimmy and Leonie.

'Close!' Jimmy gasped as they reached the corner of Woodbridge Road.

'But not a bad day out after all!' Leonie laughed.

'Avast, me hearties!' Daisy cried, leading a cutlass charge towards the park... where Winona stepped out in her shiny black shoes and stopped them.

'You owe me one!' she hissed at Daisy. 'For not telling Bernie King what I know!'

Daisy, Jimmy and Leonie stared back at Mizz Neat-and-Petite. 'Leave it out, Win-oh-na!' they cried as one.

Then, Daisy grinned, waved her invisible sword above her head and raced for the swings.

Get real, Roxanne!

One

'Witchy-woo, witchy-wee,
Cast a spell, just for me!'
Daisy Morelli practised her magic in front of
a mirror. She was getting ready for Hallowe'en
– witchy black cloak, tall pointy hat and a
broomstick. 'Haaah-ha-hah-hah!' Her cackle
was coming along nicely. She turned to
Herbie, her beanie babe hamster, who was
squatting on the bed. 'Sorry, Herb, did that
scare you?'

The hamster stared back with his one eye.
Do I look like I'm shivering in my shoes?

'Eyes of newt, ears of dog,
Turn my Herb into a frog!'

Daisy cast the powerful spell and waved her broomstick over her favourite soft toy. She frowned when Herbie stayed exactly as he was. Hmm, more practice was needed.

'So, anyway, Herb, how about you come trick-or-treating with me and Jimmy?' Daisy's lightweight witch costume flounced up as she plumped down beside him. She studied the silver-paper buckles on her special pointy witchy shoes.

'We'll be calling on all the people we know, woo-wooing through their letter-boxes, yelling, "Trick or treat!" Most of 'em settle for giving us a treat, but just in case anyone asks for a trick, Jimmy's bought stuff from the joke shop.'

Herbie's eye winked in the light.

Daisy looked down at the squidgy, half-bald hamster. 'Hey, you could come as a rat for the night!'

A rat? But I'm a hamster!

'I know.' Daisy seized a length of thick, Day-Glo-green string from her bedside table. Using one of the safety pins that held her witch costume together, she pinned the string on to Herbie's bottom. 'Now you have a tail! It's gonna be dark out there, so you'll look like a rat.'

But why a rat? Herbie still looked fed-up.

'Witches have rats!'

No, they have cats.

'Oh, shut up, Herbie, and do as you're told!' Daisy carried him across to the mirror. 'Try to look wicked and witchy, OK?' Sitting the hamster on her shoulder, she made ugly faces. 'Hah-hah-hah! Trick or treat!' she screeched.

Witch Morelli soared through the night sky with her pet rat on her shoulder. She flew amongst shooting stars and over the moon to the dark side, where she collected new spells from the Queen of Witches.

'Take care, daughter. And remember, be BAD!' the wizened old crone advised.

'I will,' Daisy promised. 'I'll be as bad as ever I can be!' With this, she cackled farewell and took off on her broomstick, heading for home. She flew the pretty route, via the North Star, then landed in the park close to her house. She threw a fork of lightning into the air and laughed as the thunder crashed.

'Witchy, witchy, witchy-woo,
Here comes a storm to frighten you!'

'Daisy, are you ready? Jimmy's waiting at the door!' Angie Morelli's voice called up the stairs.

'Coming!' Daisy gave one last look at her green face. She quickly blacked out her two front teeth with her mum's waterproof eyeliner. Finally she slotted a complete set of witchy green fingernails on to the ends of her fingers. Perfect!

'C'mon, Herbie!' Grabbing the hamster and tucking her broomstick under her arm, she shot downstairs.

'The wheels on the bus go round and round!'

Daisy's dad sang to baby Mia in the kitchen of the Italian restaurant that the family ran. The cheerful song rang out amongst the shiny steel cookers and sinks. Mia sat in her baby chair gooing and gurgling, her fat face creased by a broad smile.

When Daisy the witch rushed through, the smile vanished.

'Careful, Daisy!' Gianni warned, taking Mia into his arms. 'You're scaring the baby!'

Whoosh! Daisy zoomed on, into the Pizza Palazzo. Pumpkin lanterns sat on the counter, beside an advert for Gianni's Hallowe'en Special Pizza.

'Waaaaggghhhh!' Mia saw Daisy, opened

her mouth and cried.

Gianni followed Daisy into the restaurant. 'Now look what you did,' he protested. 'Mia and me were happy singing our bus song until a nasty green witch came along and spoiled it.'

Daisy spun around and whirled her cloak. 'What d'you think, Dad? Am I scary enough?'

'Plenty scary!' Gianni pulled a face. 'And Mia thinks so too!'

'Give the baby to me!' Hearing the rumpus, Angie dashed forward.

'Daisy, get out of here and do your witch stuff somewhere else. Oh and remember, be goo—'

'BAD!' Daisy grinned her toothless grin. 'Very, VERY BAD!'

After all, Hallowe'en was the one time in the year when Daisy Disaster Morelli was officially allowed to get into trouble!

'Wow, Jimmy!' Daisy was impressed by her best friend's costume. Jimmy stood on the pavement outside the Pizza Palazzo dressed as a monster-man with a big plastic bolt through his neck. His face was painted white and he wore wide shoulder pads under his blue Steelers jersey. A closer look at his face revealed rows of big black stitches painted across his cheek and forehead.

'I'm Frankenstein's monster,' he told her.

Not quite witchy, but it would do, Daisy thought. 'Where did you get the big nail through your neck?' she asked.

'From the joke shop, plus this fake blood, these vampire teeth and this smaller nail that just goes through your finger - see!' Jimmy held up the items one at a time.

Daisy grinned. 'Let's go!' she hissed, eager to begin. So the witch and Frankenstein's monster trotted down Duke Street. They passed the car spares shop run by Jimmy's dad, then the Late Nite food shop and the newsagents on the corner. It was six o'clock and the shops were mostly shut up for the night, but there was still plenty of light cast by the orange street lamps.

'Hey, Jimmy!' a voice called from across the street. The middle-aged man gave a friendly wave.

'Who was that?' Daisy asked, clunking her broomstick against a lamppost.

'My Uncle Pete,' Jimmy grunted. 'How come he recognised me?'

'Maybe it was your football jersey that gave it away,' she suggested. 'Like, since when did Frankenstein's monster wear a Steelers shirt?'

'Hi, Daisy!' Just then, Leonie Flowers came round the corner with Winona Jones tagging along. Leonie was dressed in a furry black cat costume with whiskers and a long tail.

'How did you know it was me?' Daisy muttered.

Leonie shrugged. 'I recognised Herbie.'

Daisy sniffed and re-settled the hamster-rat into a safer position tucked into the waistband of her trousers.

Ouch, I'm squashed! Herbie would've said if he'd been able.

'Hi, Daisy, hi, Jimmy!' Winona chirped. She wore her mum's smart black skirt and a black roll-neck jumper. Her golden curls hung loose around her shoulders. 'Leonie and I are going trick-or-treating!'

Leonie pulled a face. 'We just ran into one another,' she mumbled, obviously ashamed of Winona's pathetic witch costume. 'D'you two mind if we join in with you?'

Daisy hesitated. Winona Jones was Woodbridge Junior's biggest teacher's pet. It was hard to imagine her being any good at this witchy stuff.

'Please!' Leonie said. In other words, *Help! Don't leave me alone at*

Daisy sighed and looked at Jimmy. 'Give me the teeth!' Daisy said under her breath. Puzzled, he produced the vampire fangs from his pocket.

'On one condition,' Daisy warned. 'No, two! The first is that Winona has to swear to be very, very BAD!'

The glamorous blonde witch promised faithfully to try.

'And?' Leonie prompted, her tail wiggling each time she moved.

'Second: she has to wear these!' Daisy produced the vampire teeth with a flourish.

Winona stuck them in her mouth.

'F-f-fine with me!' she said. 'What are we waiting f-f-for? Let's go!'

Two

Kyle Peterson's mum gave the Hallowe'en visitors a chocolate biscuit each. Kyle had peered out through the front room curtains, keeping a safe distance. A bag of pick 'n' mix came from Jimmy's uncle, and some Kit-Kats from Leonie's next door neighbour. Half an hour into trick-or-treating, Daisy's gang were heavy on calories and light on loose change.

Daisy held up her carrier bag and clinked the few coins she'd managed to collect. 'Pretty stingy, huh?'

'Let's try your place next,' Leonie suggested.

'The Pizza Palazzo?' Until then, Daisy hadn't considered knocking on her own door. 'It's nearly seven o'clock. Mum and Dad could be busy by now.'

'Exactly!' Leonie grinned. 'Lots of lovely customers sitting at the tables, all in a good mood because they're out for a meal. We just swoosh in and trick-or-treat them.'

'Good idea,' Jimmy agreed, turning back. 'I bet we get loads of dosh!'

So the two witches and their cat got on their broomsticks and followed Frankenstein's monster down Duke Street. They swooped through the doors of Pizza Palazzo with a cackle and a whoosh.

The wind from the open door made the pumpkin lanterns flicker. 'Trick or treat!' Leonie cried at a romantic couple sitting at a dim corner table.

'Treat.' The man pulled a piece of gum from his top pocket and handed it over with a smile. The woman dipped into her bag to find a fifty-pence piece.

'Now we won't cast a wicked spell!' Leonie

promised, pleased by how well her idea was turning out.

'Trick!' the lady eating out with a friend chose with a smile.

Daisy made a big thing of casting a spell.

'Hubble-bubble, just you wait,

Something nasty on your plate!'

Splat! She magicked Herbie from under her cloak and plonked him squidgily on the woman's side-plate. Both diners let out a satisfying squeal until Daisy picked Herbie up by his green tail and whisked him out of sight. *Da-dah!*

'Very scary!' the first customer said with a shudder. 'For a moment, I thought it was Gianni's Hallowe'en Special!'

'I heard that!' Daisy's dad cut in. 'Now scoot, bambinos, and leave us in peaces!'

With a final whisk of her cloak and a loud cackle, Daisy

led the way back on to the street. 'How did we do?' she asked.

'Fifty pence, a piece of gum, three ten pence coins and a signed Steelers' programme,' Leonie counted up.

'Let's see!' Daisy grabbed the football match memento from Jimmy. She made out the name scrawled across the front – Kevin Crowe, the ace manager of their premiership team. 'Cool!' she breathed.

Jimmy beamed. 'Where to now?' he asked.

'Let's try a teacher's house,' Leonie suggested with a wicked gleam in her eye. 'How about Waymann herself?'

Winona's mouth fell open and she almost lost her teeth. Mrs Waymann was the headteacher of Woodbridge Junior and scarier than any witch or monster.

Jimmy too looked nervous. But Daisy took up the challenge. 'Great idea!' she said, and straightaway led the charge to Lilac Avenue.

The head's house was large and creepy. It

was surrounded by a high hedge and covered in ivy. A winding gravel drive led to an arched stone porch and a heavy, studded door.

Rat-a-tat-tat! Daisy lifted the lion-head knocker and let it fall. She took a deep breath and waited.

'No one's in!' Winona whispered in a choked voice. 'Let's go.'

'Wait a second.' Leaning her head against the door, Leonie heard footsteps. 'Someone's coming!'

The trick-or-treaters prepared to whooh and wail. The big door opened and a small man appeared.

'Whhhooo – oh!' Daisy stopped dead. The man was thin and bald with rimless glasses – a tiny, mouse-like creature.

'Wrong house!' Jimmy hissed, ready to scarper.

But then a voice they knew boomed from a back room. 'Michael, who is it? If it's that tiresome man selling vacuum cleaners, get rid of him at once!'

'No, dear. It appears to be a couple of witches and...' Mrs Waymann's mousey husband stepped aside as the headteacher surged forward. She was dressed in a white furry sweater, black trousers and soft slip-on shoes.

'Whhh-oooo!' Daisy and Leonie waved their arms and tried to keep their faces well out of sight. But, unluckily for Daisy, her hat fell off and her pile of messy black hair came into view.

'Daisy Morelli!' Waymann pounced. 'I might have known.' She seized witch number one with a grip of steel.

'Trick or treat!' Leonie stammered.

'Leonie Flowers!' The headteacher peered over the top of her glasses. 'Jimmy Black and Winona Jones!'

So much for their disguises!

'Winona, whose idea was this?' Mrs Waymann began. 'No, don't tell me, let me guess. It could only be Daisy who would dream up something so earth-shatteringly silly!'

'By my hat and by my broom,
Through the heavens let me zoom!'
Witch Morelli's spell worked in a trice.
Before she knew it, she had escaped from
the enemy's deadly grasp. Astride her
broomstick, she travelled at the speed of
light to the top of the highest mountain in
the world. An icy wind cut through her
cloak and icicles formed on the end of her
nose, but she was free!

Mrs Waymann shook Daisy by the collar. 'I'll trick or treat *you*, Daisy Morelli, for leading these other three astray!'

Mousey Mr Waymann tried to step between them. 'Erm, dear, perhaps it would be a good idea to – erm – put Daisy down.'

But Waymann shook harder than before. Daisy's plastic fingernails dropped off and Herbie fell to the floor.

Don't leave me! he pleaded silently.

Leonie picked the hamster up and backed down from the porch with Winona and Jimmy.

'S-s-s-sorry, Miss!' Daisy stammered, her teeth rattling. She felt herself go limp and cross-eyed.

'Not half so sorry as you will be tomorrow morning,' Waymann warned, finally letting go of Daisy's collar.

Daisy flopped to the floor and scuttled down the steps, leaving her green fingernails behind.

'Come to my office before assembly!' Waymann cried after her. She had to raise her voice as the gang made a run for it through the hedge into the next garden. 'Then let's see the fine mess that your silly trick-or-treating has got you into!'

Three

'Don't worry, I'll tell Waymann it was my idea,' Leonie promised.

Daisy puffed and panted to regain her breath. Her brain still rattled inside her head from the shaking she'd received. 'She won't believe you,' she gasped sulkily. 'If anything happens, she always thinks it's my fault!'

'That's because it usually *is*,' Winona pointed out primly.

'Here.' Looking sorry for Daisy, Leonie handed Herbie back to her. 'Let's work out who to trick or treat next.'

As they recovered from their Waymann ordeal, Jimmy began to make small squeaking noises. He tiptoed along the hedge *eek*ing and holding his front paws up to his chin. 'Who am I supposed to be?' he demanded.

'Mr Waymann!' Leonie giggled. 'Also known as, Mickey Mouse!'

Even Daisy smiled and began to look around. Their escape through the hedge had brought them into the garden of another large house, with a fish-pond and tall, shadowy statues of bare, naked ladies.

'Don't look!' Daisy hissed at Jimmy, slapping her hands across his eyes.

'What? Who? Where are we, anyway?' Pulling himself free, Jimmy Frankenstein braved the shameless statues.

'Actually, we're in my cousin Roxanne Fontaine's garden,' Winona told them calmly.

Leonie stared at the big white house. 'Wow, Winnie, I didn't know you had rich relations!'

'Don't call me Winnie!' Winona stuck her

nose in the air. 'My Uncle Jonathan does things with computers. My Aunty Miranda teaches aerobics.'

'Posh, or what?' Jimmy was impressed.

'So what are we waiting for?' Daisy demanded, marching straight up to the front door. She expected a mega treat from people who were mega rich. 'Let's threaten to turn their massive goldfish into tiddlers if they don't hand over the goodies!'

Leonie and Jimmy ran to catch her, but Winona hung back. 'They're not goldfish, they're koi carp. And my Aunty Miranda doesn't let Roxanne go trick-or-treating. She says it's not the sort of thing nice kids do.'

'So, who wants to be a *nice* kid?' Daisy turned to Jimmy. 'Where's your fake blood?' she asked.

Jimmy pulled it out of his pocket – a shiny, bright red splat of plastic with a sticky back.

'Who wants to wear this?' Daisy asked, choosing Winona and slapping the blood patch on to her forehead.

'Ooh, gruesome!' Leonie laughed, dragging

Winona forward to ring the doorbell.

'I really don't think we should be doing this!' she stammered.

But Jimmy put his thumb firmly on the bell for her, then stood back between Daisy and Leonie. Tip-tappety footsteps came across the hall.

'Woooo-oooo-ooooh!' Daisy, Jimmy and Leonie wailed.

Winona stood by the door, fiddling with her fake blood.

'Witchy-woo, witchy-wish,
We'll cast a spell upon your fish!'

Daisy gave one of her best cackles as slowly the door opened.

'Trick or treat!' they all cried.

The small, plump blonde girl at the door saw them. She took in Winona's fake blood, Jimmy's stitched Frankenstein face, a black cat and a tall, pointy, witch hat. Then she opened her little round mouth wide and screamed.

'Stop that, Roxanne, it's only me,' Winona said crossly. But her seven-year-old cousin went on screaming so loudly that she didn't hear. Turning deadly white, she grasped the door handle and swayed forward.

'Watch it, she's gonna faint!' Leonie warned.

'Roxy, it's me, Winona!'

'Help, someone!' Roxanne cried as she swooned to the floor.

'Typical!' Winona frowned as she watched her cousin fall in a dead faint. 'Roxy always needs to be the centre of attention!'

'Erm, what do we do now?' Jimmy wanted to know.

Daisy stared down at the heap on the floor. 'Pat her cheek,' she suggested. 'Maybe that'll bring her round again, and we can explain that we're not real witches.'

But Jimmy held back. '*You* pat her cheek!'

'Listen, someone else is coming!' Leonie had picked up sounds from upstairs.

'It's my Uncle Jonathan!' By this time, Winona too had panicked and turned pale. 'I'll get killed if he sees me!' Quick as a flash she turned and ran through the garden, past the statues, back into the deep shadows of the hedge which bordered on to the Waymanns' house.

Which left Jimmy, Daisy and Leonie gazing helplessly at Roxanne.

'We need to throw cold water over her to wake her up!' Leonie decided. She vanished in the direction of the fish-pond.

Which left just Jimmy and Daisy. Daisy fell to her knees and wafted air around Roxanne's face. She thought she saw her eyelids flicker, but there was no other movement. And the heavy footsteps were coming slowly downstairs.

'C'mon, wake up, Roxanne!' Daisy pleaded. 'Get real! We're not proper witches. This is Hallowe'en, remember!'

No sign of life – nothing! Maybe Daisy and the gang had literally scared Winona's little cousin to death!

'Her mouth twitched!' hawk-eyed Jimmy claimed.

'Where's Leonie with that water?' Daisy

hissed. For a milli-second she thought about legging it before Mr Fontaine showed up. But how would that look to the outside world?

GIRL FOUND ON DOORSTEP! A big picture of Roxanne stared out from the front page of the newspaper. Her round face was smiling at the camera and she was dressed in a frilly party dress.

'HALLOWE'EN PRANK TURNS TO TRAGEDY! Roxanne Fontaine, aged 7 years, of Lilac Avenue, collapsed after a cruel kids' hoax. Her unfeeling attackers fled the scene, but police are following up a strong lead given to them by the Fontaines' next-door neighbour and local headteacher, Judith Waymann, 49.

'"I know who committed this callous act!" Mrs Waymann told reporters. "The

*culprits called at my
house just minutes before
the fatal incident. Now
it's only a matter of time
before these heartless
monsters are caught!"'*

'What are we gonna do?' Jimmy whispered,
his eyes round with fright. 'Daisy, think of
something!'

So she did. She grabbed Roxanne by the
hands and hauled her to her feet. 'Hold on to
her a sec!' she muttered to Jimmy, whisking
off her black cloak and wrapping it around
Roxanne. She plonked her own pointed hat on
their victim's head, then ran round the back of
her. 'OK, I'll prop her up. How does she look
from the front? Dead or alive?'

'Alive – kind of,' Jimmy answered doubtfully.

'Who left this door open?' Jonathan
Fontaine yelled out as he crossed the hall.
'Miranda, Roxanne, did either of you forget to
close the door?'

'How about this?' Daisy hissed, frantically

waving Roxanne's arms from behind as if she was working a puppet.

'Better,' Jimmy admitted.

'OK, we're ready!' she gasped.

Mr Fontaine peered suspiciously into the dark night.

'Wooo-ooooh!' Daisy wailed, propping Roxanne up and waving her arms around, still careful to keep out of sight.

'Witchy-witchy-woooooh!'

Jimmy took a deep breath. 'T-t-rick or t-t-reat!' he stammered.

Daisy worked Roxanne like mad.

'Witchy-woo, witchy-wish,
We'll turn your wife into a fish!'

Four

'I didn't mean to say that spell – it just slipped out!' Daisy gasped.

She and Jimmy let Roxanne drop to the ground at Leonie's feet. Winona's cousin lay without moving, her eyes tight shut. Daisy's cloak covered most of her body.

Daisy had uttered the fish spell right in Mr Fontaine's face.

'You'll turn my wife into a – what?' he'd spluttered. Not for a moment had he suspected that he was staring at his own, possibly dead daughter!

'T-t-trick or t-t-treat!' Jimmy had stammered a second time.

'Get lost, you horrible kids!' Jonathan Fontaine had replied. Then he'd slammed the door with a loud bang.

But at least dressing Roxanne in Daisy's witch costume had worked. Once the door was closed, Daisy had told Jimmy to grab one arm and help her drag their victim out of sight. 'Quick, before they realise that their precious daughter's gone missing!'

Together they'd stumbled to join Leonie by the fish pond. And now they were staring down at a lifeless form.

'Don't even say it!' Daisy warned Jimmy before he'd had time to draw breath.

'What?' he complained.

'Don't say, "What are we gonna do now?", because I haven't the faintest idea!'

Leonie too was totally stuck. 'Maybe we'd better just own up after all.'

'Oh, yeah, dump the body back on the doorstep and admit we've scared their daughter to death!' Daisy muttered. She stooped to take back her hat and jam it on her head. As she did this, Roxanne's eyelids flickered and she moaned softly.

'See, she didn't snuff it!' Jimmy cried, as if he'd known this all along.

' 'Course she didn't, stupid!' Leonie and Daisy exclaimed together. They tutted and gave him a scornful "Huh, boys!" look.

'Uh-uh-uuuhhh!' Roxanne groaned. She turned her head and opened her eyes. Staring blankly at Daisy, Leonie and Jimmy, she sat up.

Jimmy took a step back, almost stumbling into the fish pond. 'Why does she look so weird?' he bleated.

'I expect it's because she's just coming round from being unconscious,' Leonie explained. 'Like she's still half asleep.'

'Look at her eyes!' Daisy whispered.

Roxanne's eyes had rolled crazily and ended in a squint. When she began to talk, her voice was slow and sing-song. 'Give me your orders, oh, Majesty!'

'Who? What?' Jimmy started to panic all over again.

'I think she means you!' Leonie said to Daisy, standing back hastily as Roxanne stumbled to her feet.

'Oh, Queen of the Witches, what is your command?' Roxanne chanted, raising her arms and holding them out straight in front as if she was about to walk in her sleep.

'M-m-me?' Daisy stammered. 'I'm not – I mean, you're making a mistake – we're not even real...!' To prove her point she took off her hat. 'I'm Daisy Morelli, and this is Jimmy Black and Leonie Flowers. We go to Woodbridge Junior with your cousin, Winona Jones!'

'Win-oh-na!' Roxanne wailed, tiptoeing over the smooth lawn towards the gate. 'Daisy, Queen of the Witches commands me to cut off all your go-olden cu-urls!'

'No, stop! I never said any such thing!'

Desperately, Daisy ran after her. 'Listen, Roxy, wake up! I mean, snap out of it, whatever it is!'

'This is really weird!' Jimmy said faintly.

Leonie said nothing. Instead, she stared at Roxanne.

'I think she's gone nuts!' Daisy concluded. 'Something's wrong with her brain. She really and truly thinks I'm the chief witch thingummy!'

'I know where you're hiding, Win-oh-na!' Roxanne said in her ghostly, echoing voice. 'Come out from under the hedge and have your cu-urls chopped off!'

For the first time since they'd rung the Fontaines' bell, Daisy remembered that Mizz Scaredy had scarpered. Following Roxanne along the pavement, she peered under the beech hedge and spied Winona's neat shiny shoes.

'Come out!' Roxanne wailed. 'Her Majesty is very angry. She's put a curse on you for running away!'

The hedge rustled and Winona stepped out. 'Leave it out, Roxanne!' she snapped. 'Who do you think you're trying to kid?'

Her cousin tottered, swayed and turned her back, but Winona quickly blocked her way again.

'Watch it, Winona. She fainted, then went nuts!' Jimmy warned.

Winona sighed and put her hands on her hips. 'Yeah, yeah! So what's new?'

'You mean she's done this sort of thing before?' Leonie asked, her eyes narrowing suspiciously.

'All the time. Roxanne's an expert fainter. She practises in front of a mirror.'

'You mean she's faking it! But why?' Jimmy was slow to understand.

'Yeah, and look!' Daisy wafted her hand across Roxanne's squinty gaze. Roxanne didn't blink. 'Her brain's definitely gone wonky!'

Sighing again and tutting, Winona reached out and tickled under her cousin's chin. 'She doesn't mind you waving your hand in her face, but she hates this worse than anything. Watch.'

As Winona wiggled her finger, Daisy, Leonie

and Jimmy saw Roxanne's mouth wobble.
Then she let out a noise, midway between a
splutter and a snort. Twisting away from
Winona's finger, she tripped over Leonie's foot
and landed with a bump on the pavement.

'Thanks, Winona!' she spat out. 'Trust you to
come along and spoil everything!'

'You sneaky little...!' Daisy exclaimed.

Roxanne's eyes had gone back to normal
and she was busy dusting herself down as if
nothing had happened.

'So she was awake all the time?' Jimmy
muttered. 'She faked all that fainting stuff and
the "Oh, Majesty" bit as well?'

' 'Course she did!' Winona said scornfully.
'You obviously don't know my darling little
cousin.'

'You lowdown, dirty, rotten, sneaky,
cheating, fibbing...' For once, Daisy ran out of
words.

'Yeah, but clever!' Leonie pointed out,
starting to smile. Soon a big grin had spread
across her face.

'Don't encourage her!' Winona's prim voice objected.

'You must admit, she had us fooled.' Now that Daisy was beginning to get over her shock, she too admired the trick. 'Why did you play along with us when we dressed you up to fool your dad?' she inquired.

'Simple.' Now that she was normal again, Roxanne sounded like Winona - all prim and prissy. 'Mum and Dad refused to let me go trick-or-treating, so I had to work out a secret way. When you lot came to the door and got me out of the house, that was perfect.'

'So you were never really and truly scared?' Jimmy said faintly. A frown creased his forehead.

Winona snorted and Roxanne shook her head.

'Neat!' Leonie laughed, even though the joke was on them.

'How old are you?' Daisy demanded.

'Seven,' Roxanne said proudly. 'And a quarter!'

Daisy gave a low whistle, realising that
Roxanne Fontaine had a great future ahead of
her. 'That's pretty amazing!'

'Typical!' Winona grunted, upstaged again
and she didn't quite know how.

Roxanne glowed under the praise she was
receiving. 'How was the faint? Did I fall right?'

'Yeah, excellent!' Daisy and Leonie assured
her.

'And how about the "Oh, Majesty" part?'

'Maybe a little bit over the top,' Leonie
advised.

'The eyes were good though,' Daisy added.

Poor Jimmy Frankenstein was still catching
up, but Winona was growing impatient. 'So
what now?' she nattered.

'How long have you got, Roxy?' Daisy
asked.

Roxanne glanced at her watch. 'About ten
minutes before the end of Coronation Street
and Mum and Dad realise I'm not in my
room.'

Ten minutes trick-or-treating. Daisy knew it
had to be something really special to live up

to the standard Roxanne had just set. So she gathered the group around her for a team talk. Ten minutes wasn't long. They'd already visited most of their families and friends. They wanted to do something daring which Roxy would enjoy.

'Got it!' Daisy sprang clear of the group with a shout of triumph.

'Uh-oh!' Winona recognised the wild Morelli look.

'What is it?' Leonie, Jimmy and Roxanne asked eagerly.

Daisy pointed over the tall hedge to the house with the ivy and shadowy stone porch. She didn't care if it got her into deeper trouble tomorrow. Tonight was what mattered – witches on broomsticks, wicked spells and bags of Hallowe'en loot.

'C'mon!' she whooped, eyes sparkling, sailing on the next wave of adventure. 'Let's go and scare the pants off Wicked Waymann one more time!'

Never again, Natalie!

One

'Cinderella, you shall go to the ball!' Natalie Brown waved her wand over Winona Jones's head.

Daisy yawned.

'But how can I go to the ball in rags?' Winonarella wailed.

Drrring! Fairy Godmother Natalie waved her wand a second time. Cindy's rags turned into a dream dress.

Daisy's head nodded.

'Fetch me a pumpkin and six white mice... Now place the pumpkin on the floor...'

Zzzzzzz. Daisy dozed.

'...Golden coach and six white horses!'

'Curtains!' Miss Ambler screeched. 'Close the curtains, Daisy. Now!'

She jerked awake. Whoops, she'd missed her cue for the third time in a row. Jimmy had pressed the smoke-button and the white cloud had drifted across the stage. But Daisy hadn't turned the handle to wind the curtains across. And Ambler was tearing her hair out.

The teacher stormed up on to the stage and fought her way through the cloud of white smoke. 'Daisy Morelli!' she spat out. 'Can't you do even the most simple job? Your cue to close the curtain is Natalie's line which ends "Six white horses!" We've been rehearsing this for five whole weeks, and you still get it wrong!'

'Sorry, Miss,' Daisy muttered. What else could she say? "Sorry, Miss, I was so bored by the lousy play that I fell asleep!"

'Sorry isn't good enough!' Miss Ambler screeched. 'If Jimmy can press his smoke-button on cue, I don't see why even you, Daisy, can't get your timing right!'

'Miss, don't worry, I'll remind her next time!' Jimmy promised quietly.

'This is our last-but-one rehearsal!' The teacher ranted on. 'It's the vital scene before the main interval, where Natalie waves her wand over the pumpkin and mice, the cloud of smoke fills the stage and the curtains close on the misty scene. It's the big transformation moment!'

In a way Daisy felt sorry for Rambler-Ambler. She'd worked hard on this Christmas show and got into a real tizz over it. 'Sorry,' she said again. 'It won't happen on Wednesday, I promise.'

Ambler frowned at her. She'd calmed down a bit and was starting to look sad and disappointed. Daisy squirmed under the Oh-Daisy-How-Can-You-Do-This-To-Me expression.

'Miss, can't somebody else take over from Daisy?' Winona suggested as the smoke drifted away. She obviously didn't want Daisy to ruin her big scene.

The teacher shook her head. 'It's too late for that, I'm afraid. Today's Monday and our first performance is in forty-eight hours' time. Who could learn the curtain cues in less than two days?'

'I can do it!' Daisy insisted. She might be bored out of her skull with the Christmas show, but she still couldn't face the thought of having to go home and tell her mum and dad that she'd been sacked. 'It'll be all right on the night!'

'Hmm.' Ambler sighed.

Luckily for Daisy, at that moment, the school caretaker came into the empty hall.

'Time for me to lock up!' Bernie King yelled, his white bulldog, Fat Lennox, lurking at his heels.

'Yes, thank you, Mr King!' Ambler replied crossly. 'I'm perfectly well aware of the time!'

The stocky, grumpy King of Woodbridge Junior tapped his watch. 'Seven o'clock is what it says on my timesheet. And it's now five minutes to.'

Lennox padded down the long assembly hall towards the stage like a nightclub bouncer. *When the boss says "Leave!", you leave!*

'Very well, children, let's all go home and get a good night's rest.' Miss Ambler crumpled in the face of Fat Lennox. She cast an eye over her actors – Jared playing the part of Prince Charming, Winona as Cinders, Natalie from Mrs Hunt's class as the Fairy Godmother, and not forgetting Nathan Moss as Buttons. 'You're all doing extremely well,' she told them kindly. 'And once we've got over the technical hitches – she cast a cool eye at Daisy – I really do believe that this is going to be one of the most successful

Christmas shows that Woodbridge Junior has ever put on!'

'Jimmy Black, you *shall* go to the ball!' Daisy cried, waving her invisible wand. She balanced on top of the playground wall, standing in the orange glare of the street lamp.

'Oh no, please, no!' Jimmy pleaded from the wet pavement. 'Anything but the ball!'

'Unless it's a foot-ball!' Daisy grinned, jumping down from the high wall and landing in a puddle. She and Jim had agreed to walk home to Duke Street together.

'How boring is Boring-Snoring's pantomime?' Daisy asked, trotting alongside Jimmy as they approached a row of Christmas shops.

'Mega-boring,' he agreed. 'Are your mum and dad coming to watch?'

'Yeah, worse luck. Are yours?'

'Yeah.'

'How did we get into this mess?' she

sighed, gazing into a shop window at the
Christmas lights and stacks of presents –
videos, hi-fis, widescreen TVs – if only you
were rich enough.

'Dunno.' Not only did Jimmy have to work
the smoke machine, but also the stage lights.
'But at least we don't have to stand on-stage
and say stupid lines, like Nathan.'

Daisy put on a Nathan voice. '"Cinders, I
may only be the messenger boy around here,
but believe me, I'm your best friend in the
whole wide world!"'

'Yeah, and Jared,' Jimmy agreed. '"Find me
the owner of this glass slipper and I'll make
her my bride!" Yuck!'

'Yeah, thank heavens we don't have to do that,' Daisy sighed. Then she forgot the school show and began to drool over a mini CD player she'd been dreaming about for three whole months now.

'Dress rehearsal!' Miss Ambler announced next day in her high, worried voice. She was down in the assembly hall, fussing and fretting. 'Remember, this is where we run through the whole show without stopping!'

'Yeah, and we get the afternoon off school!' Daisy grinned at Jimmy from her place by the curtain handle. This had been her main reason for volunteering in the first place, knowing that they would miss literacy hour and P.E. on the last Tuesday before Christmas.

'Is everybody in costume back there?' Ambler asked. 'Yes, Miss!' Winona piped up for all the rest. The two boys from Mr Coward's class who were playing the Ugly Sisters put on their big-hair wigs, ready to begin. They flounced up their orange and red frilly skirts and checked their striped stockings and big workmen's boots.

'Gertrude and Ermintrude, come and take up your positions on-stage,' Miss Ambler called. Her voice cracked with tension. 'And Daisy, get ready for your first curtain cue!'

Daisy yanked the handle and the curtains opened jerkily.

The two sisters galloped on to the stage, shrieking for Cinders to brush their hair and tie their shoes.

Winona stood in the wings in her ragged dress. 'Wish me luck!' she whispered to Jimmy and Daisy. Then she took a deep breath and scurried on.

Two

Zzzzz... Before Prince Charming had sent out invitations to the ball, Daisy was already dozing.

Zzzzzzz... While the sisters were getting ready, she'd fallen into a deep sleep.

'Wake up, Daisy!' Jimmy poked her in the ribs.

'Uh? Whah?' she mumbled. Still half asleep, she began to turn the handle.

'No, hold it!' Jimmy hissed. 'Natalie's just gone on. Wait for the bit about the pumpkin and the six white horses!'

'Oh yeah, thanks!' Daisy muttered. She'd been dreaming about Father Christmas bringing her the exact mini-CD player she'd seen in the shop. His kindly face had twinkly eyes and a broad smile. He was red and rosy, with a big white beard...

Zzzz... She was off again.

'Daisy, this mini-CD player is your reward for being a good child this year!' Santa told her. His elves were busy taking other presents out of the sack. Rudolph stood nearby, his red nose lighting up the sky like a beacon.

'Why, thank you, Father Christmas!' Daisy gasped in a Walt Disney, Snow-Whitey way. Bells jingled in the background, the roofs were covered in snow. Far away, a children's choir sang "White Christmas".

Daisy's eyes sparkled as she began to open her presents. There was a skateboard and a silver scooter, a widescreen TV and

'Daisy!' Jimmy jabbed her awake again.

'Now fetch me a pumpkin and put it on the floor!' the fairy godmother was saying to a puzzled Cinder-ona.

Cinders' face was smudged with ash, her feet were bare. Fairy Natalie was dressed all in glittery pink, with sparkly wings and a golden wand. Jimmy got ready to press his smoke button. Daisy gritted her teeth to stay awake long enough to wind her handle. Winona rushed offstage, grabbed a giant fake pumpkin, dashed back and dumped it at Natalie's feet.

'This will become your golden coach. Now bring me six white mice!' Fairy Natalie said.

Daisy's eyes glazed over. 'Hurry up, you two!' she muttered. She'd seen the scene so many times that it was worse than watching paint dry. Even Jimmy's finger twitched on the button, eager for it to finish.

Back came Winona for the six stuffed-felt

mice. 'Daisy, are you awake?' she hissed as she passed by. 'This is your cue. Start winding!'

Jimmy pressed and smoke whirled.

'And now, Cinderella, you *shall* go to the ball!' Natalie promised as Winona returned.

Daisy frantically wound the handle. The curtains began to jerk shut.

'Very good, everyone!' Miss Ambler called from the hall.

Onstage, thick white smoke drifted everywhere. 'Hey, I can't see!' Winona complained. 'How are we meant to find our way offstage?'

'Stop the smoke, Jimmy!' Natalie coughed and fumbled in the dark. *Crash!* She blundered into a painted screen, then, *ouch!* She stumbled, tripped and fell to the floor. 'Ohhh!' she cried. 'My ankle hurts!'

For a few moments, until the smoke cleared, there was chaos as Miss Ambler climbed on to the stage and fought her way through the curtains. Then, after a while, they could all make out poor Natalie sitting on the floor, her wings wonky, clutching her ankle with both hands.

'What happened?' the teacher gasped.

'I don't know, Miss. I think I fell over the pumpkin.'

Ambler crouched down beside her. 'How much does it hurt? Can you stand up?'

Slowly Natalie tried to move. But as soon as she put weight on the ankle, she winced and tears came to her eyes. 'I can't, Miss!'

'Oh dear!' Miss Ambler couldn't hide her worry. 'This is a disaster. What are we going to do?'

Brave Natalie tried again. But her pretty face screwed up in pain. 'Do you think it's broken?' she whispered.

'No, dear. You've probably sprained it, that's all.' Ambler tried to think clearly. 'Nathan, run to the office and ask Mrs Hannam to phone

Natalie's mum. Winona, bring a chair for Natalie to sit on. Jared, go to the kitchen and bring some ice wrapped in a tea-towel. Tell the kitchen staff that we need it for a sprained ankle. And Natalie, don't try to move any more. We'll get a doctor to look at this. He'll probably strap it up and then you'll be fine!'

Despite the teacher's soothing words, Natalie couldn't help crying. 'Miss, it really hurts!' she wailed. 'What if I can't walk by tomorrow? I won't be able to play the fairy godmother!'

'Sshh, dear. We'll worry about that later.' Miss Ambler too looked close to tears. Natalie's part in the show was important, and it seemed far too late to ask someone else to stand in for her.

Still clutching her ankle as she sat down, Natalie looked at the crowd which had gathered around. The smell of the dry-ice smoke lingered in the air and the backstage area was only dimly lit. But she was able to spy Daisy and Jimmy hovering at the edge of the group. 'Don't worry, Jimmy, it wasn't your

Definitely
101
Daisy

fault,' Natalie sobbed.

Her attempt to cheer him up only made him feel worse. 'I'm really sorry,' he told her, his freckled face pinched and worried.

She sniffed and tried to joke. 'Fancy the fairy godmother tripping over the bloomin' pumpkin!'

'But what are we going to do?' Winona was the only one who didn't smile. 'The show can't go on without you, Nats! Who can we get to play your part?'

The injured fairy frowned. She looked from one to the other of the cast and crew. Then her eyes settled on Daisy.

Daisy spotted the look and tried to melt into the background. *Beam me up! Take me on to the mother-ship! GET ME OUT OF HERE!*

'Daisy!' Natalie murmured.

Everyone turned to stare.

'Daisy?' Winonarella echoed scornfully.

'Daisy?' Miss Ambler gasped in disbelief.

No way! Daisy backed away into the wings.

'Yes, Miss!' Natalie insisted. 'She's been to all the rehearsals. She knows my lines!'

'True,' Miss Ambler said, still doubtful. She turned to see Daisy Disaster Morelli cowering in the dark.

Daisy glowered back. Her hair fell over her face in its usual tangled mess. Her school tie was crooked, her shirt splattered with ink.

'Could it possibly work?' Ambler wondered out loud. Daisy in a shiny pink, frilly dress. Daisy waving her wand and flitting around the stage with wings?

Just then, Natalie's mother burst through the backstage entrance, led by Mrs Hannam. From the school secretary's description of the accident, Mrs Brown was expecting the worst. 'Oh, you poor thing!' she cried, ready to whisk her off to hospital straight away.

As the secretary and her mum took her weight and asked her to hop towards the door, Natalie reached out and caught hold of the hem of Daisy's shirt. 'Daisy, please! You can do it!' she whispered.

'Ssshhh!' Daisy shook her head. True, she knew the lines. But having to prance about on-stage in a pink dress would kill her.

'Jimmy, if the doctor says I can't do it, you have to persuade Daisy!' Natalie pleaded. 'Tell her it's easy-peasy. You just have to smile and be kind, wave your wand, and that's it!'

'OK, I'll try to get her to say yes,' Jimmy muttered.

Traitor! Daisy felt like she'd been stabbed in the back.

They all watched Natalie leave with a hollow feeling in the pits of their stomachs.

'Daisy Morelli?' Rambler-Ambler mused through narrowed eyes. She turned Daisy around on the spot – once, twice, three times. 'Suppose we cleaned you up and brushed your hair... maybe, just maybe it could work!'

Three

Daisy stared at the mirror in the girls' dressing room. *Huh, huh, and double-huh!* She folded her arms crossly. How – like, how on earth – had this happened? She was wearing THE DRESS! Natalie's fairy godmother costume. It was even worse than she thought. Shinier, frillier – pinker!

'You look fine,' Miss Ambler assured her.

'Everyone will laugh,' Daisy grunted.

'Why? They didn't laugh at Natalie, did they?'

'No. That's because she's Natalie and I'm

me.' Daisy still didn't quite know how she'd been press-ganged into this. She thought back to four hours earlier, when Natalie had pleaded and begged for Daisy to take over her role in the play.

'Go on, Daisy, please! My ankle is never going to get better in time for tomorrow, I just know!'

'I can't!' Daisy had whispered.

'Why not?'

'I've got a sore throat.'

'Since when?'

'It just came on about half an hour ago,' she'd croaked.

Natalie had refused to believe her.

'Come on, love, let's get you to the hospital,' her mum had insisted. 'Miss Ambler will sort something out.'

But Natalie wouldn't leave. 'Daisy, this is important! We can't let the school down!'

Yeah, we can, Daisy had thought. *Easy.*

'All the others are relying on you!'

Daisy had given the group dark looks. *No way am I doing this, OK!*

'The mums and dads are coming to watch. We can't let them down!'

Want to bet?

'Natalie, please, we have to go!' Mrs Brown had sighed.

Yeah, go! Daisy had thought. *Don't keep on looking at me like that. I'm not even taking any notice!* She'd tried her best to ignore the pleading stare from Natalie's big brown eyes. But it got to her in the end.

'OK, OK!' she'd yelled as Mrs Hannam and Mrs Brown carted Natalie off in tears. 'I'll do it!'

Everyone had gasped, except Winona, who'd tutted.

Natalie had turned one last time. 'You will? Promise?'

'I said, I'll do it,' Daisy had mumbled, regretting it straight away. A vision of the PINK dress had reared up in front of her. 'You owe me one!'

she'd called after Natalie. 'I'm only doing this as a favour to you, remember. And I'm telling you here and now, "Never again!" OK?'

And now she was well and truly cornered. She was in the dressing-room alone with Miss Ambler and Winona. A late rehearsal specially for Cinderella and the Fairy meant that Daisy was forced to miss EastEnders. And the first thing they did to her was to put her in THE DRESS. (Daisy never wore dresses. She went to birthday parties in trousers and a top, with a home-made bracelet and wacky nail varnish.)

'They itch!' she complained as Ambler secured the wings to her back. (Once, in the Infants Class, she'd been an octopus in a play called *The Sea-bed*. That was the one and only time she'd been asked to act on a stage. She'd whacked the dolphins with her tentacles and upset the mermaids. The teachers at the time had vowed, "Never again!")

'Hmm, the dress is a little big,' Miss Ambler commented. 'Never mind, I can take the seams in.'

Daisy scowled into the mirror. In the reflection she saw Jimmy sneak up to the dressing-room door. 'Don't you dare laugh, Jimmy Black!' she snarled.

Jimmy, who had turned up to work the smoke machine, did his best to keep a straight face. 'You – look – cool!' he said in a choking voice.

She turned to face him, arms folded, clutching her glittery gold wand. 'How would you like it if they put you in this horrible dress?'

He shook his head. 'I wouldn't. But then, I'm a boy!'

'So?' Daisy was beyond reason. 'It's just as bad for me!'

'Daisy, stop wittering and stand still while I put pins in the seams,' Ambler cut in.

Nearby, Winona smirked at Daisy's misery.

'Don't worry if you forget your lines,' she told her sweetly. 'I can always ad-lib.'

'Add – what?' Jimmy piped up.

'Ad-lib. Make it up as I go along,' said super-confident Barbierella. 'All Daisy really has to do is stand there and wave her wand.'

Free from the teacher's sharp pins at last, Daisy rounded on Winona. 'I won't forget my lines!' she snapped.

'Want to bet?' Winona shot back.

'Yeah, five pounds.'

'Done!'

'Girls, girls!' Miss Ambler broke in with a clap of her hands. She looked frayed at the edges, worn down by stress. Her long brown hair hung limp, and there were panda smudges under her eyes where her mascara had run. 'This is getting us nowhere,' she bleated.

As the teacher led the way on to the stage, Daisy hung back behind Jimmy and Winona. *I can't believe I'm doing this!* she said to herself, unable to bear the thought of what people would say.

Did you see Daisy in that stupid fairy costume?

Yeah, Daisy in a pink dress! With wings!
You'd never get me doin' that!
Me neither! Not for a million pounds!

'Come along, Daisy!' Miss Ambler nattered. She gave her a final shove onstage.

Daisy saw that Jimmy was already poised by his button. 'Go easy on the smoke!' she muttered, before turning to Winona sobbing her heart out among the cinders.

'Cinderella, you shall go to the ball!' Fairy Godmother Daisy said between firmly gritted teeth.

'Herbie, it was even worse than I thought!' Daisy confided in her beanie babe hamster. She'd got back home after the rehearsal in a foul mood with the world. Not even her dad's cooking or her mum's sympathetic smile had cheered her up.

'But the Fairy Godmother is a nice part,' her

mum had said. 'And at least you don't have to be on for long. A quick flick of your wand and you're off!'

'Cheer up, Daisy *mia*!' her dad, Gianni, had cried. He chucked garlic and herbs into a frying pan and stirred. 'We're proud of you to be the fairy!'

'Hmph!' Daisy had shaken her head and trudged off to bed. Now she was telling the story to soft, squidgy, one-eyed Herb. 'It was mega, mega horrible!'

Herbie stared at her from the pillow.

'Winona pushed me around all the time and Jimmy blew smoke in my eyes. Plus, I got the words mixed up!'

It could happen to anyone, Herbie's calm, cock-eyed gaze seemed to say.

'You know when your tongue sticks to the top of your mouth and the sound won't come out properly? Well, it was like that.'

I know exactly what you mean!

'Winona laughed in my face!' Daisy's stomach churned at the memory.

Forget her. She's not worth it. Herbie's squishy hamster face took on a wise expression.

'You're right. Since when did I care what Win-oh-na Stupid Jones thought? But the dress, Herbie. I mean, the DRESS!'

Herbie frowned. *I know what you're saying.*

'It's pink and it's too big. The wings itch!'

Herbie tutted. *I'll be thinking of you when you're out there waving that wand.*

Daisy snuggled into bed and stared across

the pillow at him. 'Thanks, Herbie,' she said softly.

That's OK. Goodnight.

Her eyes closed. She knew she could always rely on Herbie at times like this. 'G'night,' she sighed. 'Sleep well.'

Four

Smoke drifted into Daisy's dreams that night. Wisps of white smoke floated before her eyes, becoming thicker, turning grey and then black. Soon sparks flew and flames began to flicker.

'Fire!' a voice cried. 'Help!'

'Call the Fire Brigade!' someone else yelled. 'The whole street is ablaze and it's spreading fast!'

The firefighters battled the flames but soon the city was engulfed. Daisy coughed. Luckily she had escaped the *flames. She looked down from a hill. She was saved. The show couldn't go on now.*

Then a third voice called out that an earthquake was about to split the country in two.

There was a roar and the ground yawned open at her feet. She grabbed Herbie and fled.

'Volcano!' A man pointed to the horizon, where a mountain was spewing out ash and fire. The molten lava rolled towards Daisy in a bright red river of death.

She woke up with a start. Her heart raced, she was covered in sweat, but Herbie was fast asleep on the pillow.

Phew! Her bedside clock said 3.00 a.m. There were no fires or earthquakes, thank heavens. But then again, the stark truth stared her in the face – Daisy still had to play the Fairy Godmother.

She gazed up at the dark ceiling. How

could she get out of it? What was the one thing that would put a stop to the performance?

How about assassinating Winona?

Daisy whipped her head around to look at Herbie. 'Did you say something?'

His eye winked in a glimmer of light from the landing. *A quick, neat murder. And, bam! No Cinderella!*

Curtains for Winona. The golden curls were dull and lifeless. Her spirit was snuffed. No more Mizz Neat and Petite! Daisy sat up in bed, willing it to happen.

Get real! Herbie told her sternly. *That's just make-believe. Winona's not going to snuff it, no way. So get some more shut-eye and be ready for tomorrow. BE VERY READY. THE PERFORMANCE IS ABOUT TO BEGIN!*

Wednesday dawned cold and cloudy.

'It looks like snow,' Angie said over a breakfast which Daisy couldn't eat.

Yeah, a blizzard! She pushed her plate to one side. *Two metres of snow, please! Close the school, cancel the show!*

'No, the TV weathergirl says it will get hotter,' Gianni added. 'Daisy *mia*, what time does *Cinderella* begin tonight?'

'Seven o'clock,' she sighed. Still she clung to the possibility of snow. After all, the weather people often got it wrong.

She left the house and looked up at the heavy grey sky. 'Pray for snow,' she told Jimmy as they met up outside his doorway.

'No way,' he told her. 'The Steelers play Man U tonight. It's a big match.'

'Which we won't be able to watch,' Daisy said glumly.

Feathery snow did in fact begin to fall as they walked to school. But it soon turned to cold, wet splodges of rain.

Then, to add to the misery, Leonie Flowers greeted Daisy and Jimmy at the main entrance.

'What's this about you being in the

pantomime?' she asked Daisy. 'I thought you were working the curtains?'

'I was. But Natalie hurt her ankle,' she replied. Then she stopped in her tracks. 'Hey, wait a sec! Maybe Natalie's ankle is better and she can play the Fairy Godmother after all!'

The idea hit her out of nowhere. Why hadn't she thought of that before? Of course Natalie was better! They wouldn't need a stand-in. *Phew!*

'Daisy, wait!' Leonie called after her as she scooted towards Mrs Hannam's office. 'I just overheard Hannam talking to Mrs Brown on the phone...'

Daisy burst in on the school secretary. 'Mrs Hannam, I need to know how Natalie Brown is. Is she better? Did her mum get in touch?'

The secretary smiled her lipsticky smile. 'That's very nice and considerate of you to ask, Daisy. It means you're showing concern for others. Well done.'

'Yeah, but how's Natalie?'

Mrs Hannam arranged the registers in a neat pile then tottered over on her high heels to answer the phone.

Daisy couldn't wait any longer for her answer. She bounded in front of Mrs Hannam, her dark hair flying. 'Is Natalie coming to school today?'

'Ah well, as for that, no I'm afraid not.' The secretary swept Daisy aside with a manicured hand. 'Hello, Woodbridge Junior here, Mrs Hannam speaking!' she said into the phone.

'N-n-no?' Daisy stammered in disbelief.

'N-O, no!' Hannam repeated, one hand over the phone. 'The doctor at the hospital X-rayed her ankle and told her to stay off school for at least a week. Apparently she's sprained it very badly indeed.'

'I could've told you that,' Leonie said to Daisy during registration.

'That's it. I've had it.' Daisy was left without hope, until another sudden idea flashed through her mind. 'Hey, Leonie!' she hissed as Ambler called the register.

'Jimmy Black!'

'Yes, Miss Ambler!'

'What?'Leonie whispered back, under the cover of her school bag which was perched on her desk.

'Natalie Brown!' Boring-Snoring called.

'Absent, Miss!' Winona piped up.

Away, missing, not at her desk! Daisy leaned over to persuade Leonie 'Why don't *you* take Natalie's part in the play? You'd be really good at it. And the lines are dead easy to learn.'

'And get to wear that disgusting pink dress? You must be joking!' Leonie said.

'Leonie Flowers!'

'Yes, Miss Ambler!'

'*Oh please!*' Daisy whined.

'Winona Jones!'

'Here, Miss Ambler!'

'No way!' Leonie mouthed back at Daisy.

'Daisy Morelli!'

'Pleee-eeeease!' she begged.

'Not a chance!'

'Daisy!' Miss Ambler looked up sharply. 'Oh good, you're here,' she grunted. 'Not paying attention, as usual, I see!'

'Sorry, Miss!' Daisy croaked.

'What's wrong with your voice?' The teacher sat, pen poised.

'Miss, I've got a sore throat.' OK, so she'd tried this one before, but she was desperate. 'I've got a rash everywhere. Miss, I think I've got measles or chickenpox!'

'Nonsense, Daisy.' Ambler didn't even get up from her seat to check. 'I'm sure you're perfectly healthy.'

'Miss, I don't feel well!' she wailed feebly. 'Honest!'

Daisy lay on her deathbed in a damp attic room. The rain lashed against the small, dirty window-pane. In the grate the last embers of a miserable fire finally died.

*With cracked lips and trembling body,
Daisy spoke her last words. 'Tell Mamma
and Papa that I love them!' she whispered,
tears trickling down her poor, thin face.
'And baby Mia as well!'*

'Daisy Morelli, save your play-acting for
tonight!' Miss Ambler barked.

The rest of the kids had begun to titter and
giggle, so the teacher raised her eyebrows
and included them in her little joke. 'And let's
all hope that Daisy remembers her cues this
evening better than she answers the register
in class!'

Five

Daisy peeped through a small crack in the stage curtains. She could see people filing into the assembly hall and sitting down in the rows of seats. Mrs Waymann, the headteacher, was dressed in a purple suit, greeting families at the door.

'Daisy, come away!' Winona whispered from behind her back. 'Let someone else have a turn!'

'Hang on. I'm trying to find Mum and Dad. Yeah, here they come now!' She spied her own family shaking hands with Wicked

Waymann and making their way to the front row. Her beaming dad carried Mia, showing the baby off to all their friends.

Daisy sighed. Wow, were they in for a disappointment when she showed up as the Fairy Godmother and made an idiot of herself!

'Daisy, let me see!' Winona pestered. 'Go and get your costume on. We start in ten minutes!'

Reluctantly she stood aside and trailed off to the girls' dressing room.

'Ah, there you are!' Ambler seized her and shoved the DRESS into her arms. 'Hurry now. I want you in costume before the curtain goes up, even though you're not on until the end of the first half.'

Daisy squirmed her way through frills and flounces into the dreaded garment. It was tighter than before, and the wings felt scratchier. 'Miss, I can't breathe!' she complained.

Miss Ambler's thin patience wore out. 'Daisy, once and for all, whatever excuses you try to make, however much you scowl and look fierce, you are going onstage as Winona's Fairy Godmother. Got it?'

Daisy's scowl deepened. There must be a law against forcing kids to act parts they didn't want to act, she thought.

'Got it?' Ambler shrieked again, eyes blazing.

'Yes, Miss!' She stood to attention and wiped the scowl off her face. Ambler could be scary when she wanted.

'Good. Now go next-door and ask Mrs Hunt to put on your make-up.'

'Make-up?' Daisy echoed faintly.

Miss Ambler glared. 'Yes. Make-up. Now. Go!'

Daisy quick-marched down the corridor, wings flapping limply. She sat in silence as Mrs Hunt slapped gooey stuff over her face.

At one point Jimmy popped his head around the door, spotted her and told her the latest score. 'Man U – 1, Steelers – 2!' he crowed. 'I'm listening to it on my Walkman!'

Before he skipped off again, Mrs Hunt collared him to ask how the show was going. 'OK,' Jimmy shrugged. 'The Ugly Sisters are bossing Winona around to help them get ready for the ball.'

Laughter from the audience told Daisy that they were lapping up the comic scene. Her stomach churned and her mouth felt dry. Right now she couldn't remember a single word she was supposed to say.

'Hey, you're shaking!' Jimmy pointed out. 'Never mind, so was Winona when she went on.'

'It's only stage fright,' Mrs Hunt told them, running a brush through Daisy's mop of hair. Then she stood her up and aimed her towards Jimmy. 'Make sure she gets to where she should be, waiting in the wings for her cue,' she instructed with a weary sigh. 'I'm going to the staffroom to lie down.'

So Jimmy guided a shell-shocked Daisy along the corridor. With trembling legs and knocking knees she arrived backstage. 'How long before I go on?' she whispered in a hoarse voice.

'Soon,' Jimmy hissed back, pointing to a copy of the script. 'Gertrude and Thingummy have gone off, leaving Cinders crying in the ashes. Nathan-Buttons is just telling her that he'll always be her friend – Yuck! – now he's finished. The stage is empty except for Winona. Go on, Daisy, it's you!'

'Cinderella, you *shall* go to the ball!' Daisy swept on-stage. Music twinkled in the background and the stage lights flickered silver and gold.

Winonarella looked up from her tears at a mysterious figure dressed in pink. She stood and approached her Fairy Godmother. The audience held their breath. And held it some more.

'Go on then!' Daisy whispered to Winona out of the corner of her mouth.

Winona stood with her back to the audience, a look of terror on her face. 'I can't,

I've forgotten my lines!' she gasped.

'You say, "Who are you?"' Daisy prompted.

'W-w-who are you!' Winonarella stammered.

'Never you mind!' Fairy Daisy replied, whooshing her wand. 'Don't cry any more, Cinders. We must clean you up and get you ready for the Prince's party!'

Another look at Winonarella's terrified face told Daisy that she'd lost the plot. Her eyes were vague and starey, her lips were trembling. Whoops, Winona had stage fright big-time!

So Daisy cleared her throat and began to order her around. *Drring!* She waved her wand and whipped off Cinders' cloak to reveal a glittering ball gown beneath.

'Ooh!' the audience gasped.

'Bravo!' Gianni called from the front row.

'Now fetch me a pumpkin!' Fairy Daisy commanded.

It was the cue for Jimmy's smoke-button, but he was so busy listening to the footie on the radio that he missed it. *No smoke!*

Winona tripped off-stage for the fake pumpkin and ran anxiously back. As she dropped it at Daisy's feet, it rolled slowly but surely towards the edge of the stage.

Spotting the mishap, Daisy ran and niftily dribbled the pumpkin back into position while she sent Winona for the six stuffed white mice.

People in the audience tittered at her neat piece of footwork.

Meanwhile, the heroine of the show vanished again. Daisy saw Winona scrabble in the wings for the mice and panic when she couldn't find them.

Great: no smoke, no mice! And then the pumpkin wobbled and rolled a second time.

In the wings, Winona burst into tears.

'Curtain!' an invisible Miss Ambler hissed,

swallowed up by the chaos. 'Quick someone, close the curtain!'

But Daisy was intent on saving the pumpkin. She darted to the edge of the stage and scooped it up before it fell on to the people in the front row. When she turned around, she saw the curtains swish closed, leaving her all alone on the stage.

'Uh-hum!' She turned again to face the audience, pumpkin in hand. The lights dazzled her and for a moment she thought of scarpering – *Exit, stage right.*

But then something weird came over her and she felt she had to explain. 'Uh-hum!' she coughed. 'Ladies and gentlemen, this is the bit where we should have had the smoke. That was Jimmy's job, but Steelers were winning 2 – 1, and he got caught up in the match.'

'Steelers, Steelers!' the fans in the crowd chanted, then applauded.

Daisy held up her free hand for silence. 'Then Winona went for the mice, which were meant to change into six white horses for the coach to take Cinderella to the ball,' she explained carefully. 'Only, the mice weren't there, so she couldn't come back on. Then she got worked up about it and I had to save the pumpkin, which was meant to turn into a coach while the stage was filled with smoke. Only we couldn't do that either because there was no smoke, so Miss Ambler said to close the curtains quick...'

Daisy paused for breath and took in the rows of faces below her. She came over hot and sticky when she realised that every eye was turned on her in her DRESS.

'Anyway,' she faltered, backing away, wishing a hole would open up and swallow her. 'Now it's the interval, so could you please all go to the dining hall and have coffee!'

There was an awkward silence. No one moved. Then Gianni stood up with Mia in the front row. 'Bravo, Daisy *mia*!' he cried. 'Well done, *bambino*!'

'Yes indeed, well done, Daisy!' Mrs Waymann stood up too. She invited the audience to clap. 'Thanks to our Fairy Godmother, we now know what to expect in the second half!'

'Nice one, Daisy!' someone yelled from the back of the hall.

Soon other people were clapping and cheering her.

Wow! Daisy could hardly believe her eyes and ears. She grasped the pumpkin in both hands and took a bow, wings flapping around her head.

'Dai-sy, Dai-sy!' the football supporters chanted.

'Coffee, everyone!' Mrs Waymann cried, shooing them out of the hall.

As the applause died away, Daisy saw her mum and dad give her a big thumbs-up. Baby Mia waved her fat fists.

'Thank you, thank you!' she said to all her fans, smiling and backing smoothly through the gap in the curtains.

'Daisy, you're an absolute star!' Backstage, Miss Ambler seized the pumpkin, hugged her and fussed over her. 'You saved the show with your speech. The audience loved you!'

'They did?' Daisy's stomach was still
churning. She squirmed free of the teacher's
embrace.

Then she spotted Winona drying her eyes in
a dark corner. She went across. 'You OK now?'
she muttered awkwardly. Daisy knew she
wasn't big on sympathy.

'Fine,' Winonarella sniffed.

'Will you be able to carry on with the
second half?'

'I said I'm fine, I'm over it!' Winona insisted.
She flounced up her ball dress and fluffed out
her curls. 'I don't know what came over me.'

'Did your knees knock and your stomach tie
itself in knots?' Doctor Daisy checked the
symptoms.

Winona took a deep breath and nodded.

'Stage fright,' Daisy explained. 'So, we all
know this is a game of two halves!' she said
in a TV Commentator's drawl, using her wand
as a microphone. 'New signing, Cinderella,
didn't perform at anything like her best in the

first forty-five minutes, but this girl definitely has what it takes to come out fighting after the break!'

From his stool by the smoke machine, a guilty-looking Jimmy broke into a smile. 'Steelers won 3 – 1!' he whispered gleefully.

'So now maybe you can concentrate on the show.' Daisy grinned back at him. Then she turned to Winona. 'Ready?' she asked, as a big gold, cut-out coach was wheeled into place.

The stagelights went up, and out in the hall, the audience returned from their coffee break.

Winona squared her shoulders and nodded.

Hurriedly Daisy ffluffed her own pink frills and straightened her wings. 'How do I look?' she asked.

'You look great!' Winonarella smiled at her as the curtains jerked back. 'Oh, and thanks, Daisy!'

Daisy waved her wand and the music *drrringed*. The lights made the sequins on her wings sparkle. 'Cinderella, the time has come!' she announced in a clear, Fairy Godmother voice. *Hey, I'm really enjoying this! Acting's not bad, and even the DRESS isn't all that yucky... Well, maybe that's going a bit too far...*

The silver spotlight rested on her as she spoke her final lines. 'Your carriage awaits!' she said kindly to a beaming Cinderella.

Winona swished into the coach and Daisy waved her wand. Then she turned to the audience, winked at Mia and vanished in a puff of smoke.

Look out for other Definitely Daisy adventures!

Just you wait, Winona!

Jenny Oldfield

Winona's a goody goody who sticks like glue and threatens to ruin Daisy's street cred. Daisy can't deal with a teacher's pet hanging around – until classmate Leonie invites her to convert Winona into one of the gang. It's a hard challenge – but Daisy's determined to try...